Praise for the Writing of Jan McCanless'

"In these days of stress we can all use a good laugh! This book is bound to make you smile and laugh. Jan's quirky sense of humor and outlook on life will do just that! So forget your troubles, kick your shoes off, sit back and enjoy this delightful read!" —Marie Norway, Author, singer, songwriter, radio and TV personality

"McCanless is a well-known, award-winning humorist yes, but her reflections are insightful and her humor is iconic, contemporary and inspirational. She has a knack for getting us all to laugh at ourselves as we agree with her timeless truths. My go-to read." —Sherry Rentschler, bestselling author of *Time and Blood*, Book 1, Evening Bower Series

"Jan McCanless writes with humor, and Southern flair that makes her mysteries even more fun to read."—Author Marni Graf, writer of the Nora Tierney and Truly Genova Manhattan series

"Jan McCanless has the uncanny ability to spin a yarn that is not only enjoyable, but, a good, easy read, perfect for a lazy day in front of a roaring fire, or a crashing wave at the ocean. I have spent a goodly number of hours at the beach, which I am sure is close to Beryl's Cove, immersed in her delightful stories." —Camille Jones, retired ESL Teacher

"My favorite author, yours too after reading one of her books!" — Robert G. Hyers, retired engineer, Scientific Atlanta

Empower

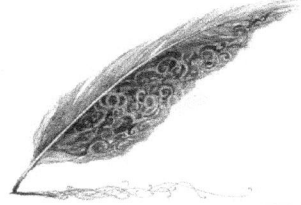

Publishing

Death in New Orleans

By

Jan McCanless

Empower Publishing
Winston-Salem

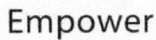

Empower

Publishing

Empower Publishing
PO Box 26701
Winston-Salem, NC 27114

First Empower Publishing Books edition published December, 2024

Empower Publishing, Feather Pen and all production design are trademarks.

For information regarding bulk purchases of this book, digital purchase and special discounts, please contact the publisher at publish.empower.now@gmail.com

Cover design by Pan Morelli

Manufactured in the United States of America
ISBN 978-1-63066-613-2

To Bob, who is always helpful, and my biggest fan.

—Jan McCanless

Author's Note

Having been to New Orleans several times, I can tell you it's a wonderful and strange place. Every city has it's dark side, and, the Crescent City is no exception.

If you have never seen one of the murkier bayous that surround New Orleans, you have no idea how formidable they can be. Teeming with wildlife, they pose a hazard to anyone traversing them. Trees growing out of the water, heavily laden with moss, make a spooky backdrop for someone foolish enough to tread the backwaters of the city. Only the most experienced of guides go this far into the bayous, and they don't stay long.

Even in this day and age, certain mulattoes and other indigenous folks practice an old timey voodoo, and it's not for the faint of heart. Not at all. In fact, it can be downright dangerous.

Don't go there

This book of fiction is loaded with fearsome and evil characters, but for the most part it will give you a flavor of Mardi Gras, truly a special festival.

So if you go, stay on your toe. Be aware and afraid—be very afraid!

Steve and Suzanne are back, in their most exciting adventure yet. During the height of Mardi Gras, Steve's niece, Cassie, disappears. Called away from the races in Kentucky, Steve and Suzanne are asked by Cassie's twin, Susie, to help find the girl.

Their search leads them down the back alleys and the deepest part of the bayou, where they encounter danger and murder.

Come with us now as our favorite sleuthing couple uncovers a murder plot so dastardly, with national repercussion. It will amaze and terrify you.

Prologue

The man paddled silently through the bayou, looking neither right nor left, at one point getting tangled up in the moss hanging from the trees. It was dusk, and a gloomy February day was ending.

Mardi Gras was in full swing but the sounds of the crowds and reveling went unheard deep in the bayous of Louisiana. A small alligator swam past, ignoring the man, and his cargo. From off to his left, towards the bank, an owl hooted, but otherwise there was no sound.

He rowed silently, finally coming upon a dilapidated dock that was built out over the water. He tied up his small boat and, lifting a blanket from the bottom, he swung it over his shoulder and climbed out. He made his way up to the dark cabin ahead, and, kicking open the door, dropped the blanket on the floor, where he pushed it to the wall. Rolled up inside was a young man, quite dead.

He was slightly built, wire-rimmed glasses rested on his nose, and, the pencil thin moustaches was beaded with sweat from the exertion of carrying a dead body up a low incline to the cabin. He sat in the only chair inside the biggest room and looking at his "cargo," contemplated what to do with him.

It wasn't supposed to end this way. He had a plan all worked out, but something went wrong and now he and the others were stuck with a corpse and no idea

1

what to do with it.

The man, the one everyone else called the "Professor," looked out the dirty window to the water. It was fast getting dark and, with no electricity in the cabin, he knew he had to start back while he could still make out the stumps, trees and other hazards that dotted the banks of the bayou. Quickly, he covered the man back up, pushed him further into the corner, and, taking a flashlight from his pocket, he made his way back down to the dock, shoved off and headed back to New Orleans.

Part 1

Chapter 1

Steve and Suzanne sat in the owners' lounge of the racetrack. They had come to Kentucky to see some of Great Scott's offspring and grandchildren run in races. Steve's racehorse had been a profitable investment, and now the granddaughters and grandsons of the big horse were winning races.

Celebrating their anniversary just a little late, they had been in Kentucky two weeks, enjoying the early racing season and visiting with some of the other owners. The lounge was busy this day, the last day of racing for the week.

The waiter had just refilled their iced tea and put piled high roast beef sandwiches in front of the Thomases, when Steve's phone pinged. He scrolled through and chuckled as he showed Suzanne a photo Rainey had taken of Dawg and Elvis romping with Skanks pet goat Dolly out on their island. He smiled at the picture of their pets rolling around on the ground, with Dolly bleating her approval.

"I'll be glad to get back to them, won't you? I miss them as much as they miss us. Steve? Hello? Are you listening?"

"Hmm?" He put his phone down and scowled at his wife. "Sorry hon, I just got a disturbing text from Susie. You up for a trip to New Orleans?"

"New Orleans? Sure, but why?"

"Seems one of the twins is missing. Susie just texted that their vacation was going well and suddenly Cassie has disappeared. She's looked everywhere for her and even contacted the police, but the girl is nowhere to be found."

"Oh my God, Steve. I don't care how old those girls are, Gene and Cassie should never have let them go to New Orlen by themselves. They're mere babies."

Steve's brother and sister-in-law had twin girls, twenty-one years old, and after their college graduation at midterm in January, they decided to take a trip to New Orleans for Mardi Gras. Both girls were now in a master's degree program, hoping to get their master's in law enforcement, while they worked part time for the Beryl's Cove Police Force.

Throwing money on the table for their lunch, Steve grabbed Suzanne by the hand and pulled her up. Headed for the door, waving to some of the other owners as they left, Steve told her they'd turn in the rental car, fly to New Orleans, and get another rental.

"C'mon, Susie will meet us at the airport, and we'll go from there."

"Has she told their parents?" Suzanne asked, running to keep up with her husband.

"Doesn't want them told until we can get together and assess the situation."

***

At the airport, they were met by their niece, rented a car, and found out the only available hotel room during Mardi Gras was on the 14th floor of the Hilton. They quickly unpacked and sat down to talk with Susie.

"Where were you and what were you doing when Cassie disappeared?"

Wiping a tear from her eye, the girl sniffled and told them they were at Pat O'Brien's when Cassie got up to us the rest room and never came back. I went to the police, but they didn't seem all that worried, and I have heard nothing more from them."

"Okay, did she leave her handbag with you? Let's see it."

Steve shook out the contents of the small bag, everything tumbling onto the bed, and looked thoroughly at the comb, ID card, wallet, tissue and hotel key that lay scattered on the bed. Her cell phone didn't reveal anything either.

"Not much here," he said, shaking his head. "C'mon. Let's go see the police chief."

***

The police department that handled the French Quarter was located in a low, nondescript building on Canal Street, with a smallish sign in front announcing it as the police station. The officer/receptionist said the Chief's name was Jaques Rochambeau, and after announcing their presence to the man, nodded that they could go right in. Shaking hands, the three Thomases sat in chairs facing the chief's desk.

Rochambeau was a tall, lanky fellow, a native of the area and police chief for only three months. "Now," he said, "What can I do for you folks?"

Leaning forward, Steve began, "My niece here tells me her sister has disappeared. The Police Department was told about it and I would appreciate knowing what all you have found out so far.

"I see, what does you sister look like Miss?"

"I'm Suzanne, Susie. My sister, Cassandra, Cassie, is my identical twin." She went on to relate about their evening at Pat O'Brien's, and how her sister just seemed to vanish into thin air." She dabbed at her eyes again. "I reported it here that very night, but no one seemed concerned. Are you even looking for her?"

Rochambeau shifted in his chair, spoke into the intercom, and summoned Officer Delaney from the front desk: "what do we know about this, Gracie?"

"Gracie Delaney shook her head. "Not much, Chief. Didn't I hear it said that the report was filed at night?"

Rochambeau thumbed through his rolodex and looked up at his officer. "Pete Reynolds is the one on night duty. Get him here, Gracie, if you would."

He looked at his guests. "Now then, can I get you all some coffee or tea while we wait?"

Drinks declined, Steve sat tapping his foot while the police chief handled some paper work. Five minutes passed and Officer Delaney returned, shaking her head. "Sorry, Jacques. Pete's gone fishing for the day and his wife doesn't know where. Only that he'll be back in time to go come to work."

"Well, there you have it, folks. When Officer Reynolds comes on duty, I'll check with him and get back to you. I do have some things to take care of now, so if you'll excuse me."

The Thomases all gave him a quizzical look and left the office more bewildered than when they came in. Out in the lobby, Grace checked to see if anyone else was around, and motioned for Steve to approach her desk.

"Mr. Thomas," she whispered, "your niece isn't the only one who has disappeared of late." Again, she looked around the lobby and up at the security monitor on the wall. "Come with me, please." She led them to a rather dark corner of the room. "Often times these local characters see and hear things that are not told to us. One woman in particular has the pulse of the community and all the darker side of the French Quarter. Her name is Mother Rosalie, and she works the front desk at the Wax Museum. Go see her," she hissed, then quickly returned to her desk.

Chapter 2

Thoroughly disgusted with the response from the local constabulary, the Thomas family walked into the New Orleans Wax Museum loaded with grit and determination.

The museum was located two blocks from the French Quarter. They noticed the parking lot had only a few cars in it. Once inside, it was easy to spot "Mother Rosalie." Sitting behind the desk, was what people used to refer to as an "ample" woman. Decked out in a flowery turban and matching caftan, she had a jewelry store's worth of bangles and beads around her throat and wrists.

She grinned at them, flashing a gold tooth in the process. "May I help you?"

Steve stepped forward and shook her limp hand. "We were told you know a lot about what goes on in this town. We're looking for a missing girl." He pointed to Susie. "Looks like her, a twin. Went missing several days ago,"

Her eyes became mere slits in her face and she jangled several bracelets. "Who told you that?" she barely whispered.

Leaning across her desk, Steve gave her a hard stare back. "Officer Delaney at the police department, if you must know. What difference does it make who told us? Do you or don't you know anything?"

9

The gypsy woman softened and smiled at the group. "Yes, Gracie. Lovely child. Now what about your niece?"

"She's missing. Disappeared from Pat O'Brien's two-and-a-half days ago. We want to find her."

"Of course you do. Hmm, let me see. That would be Andre's territory. He works there and is in charge of missing girls." Smiling at him, Mother Rosalie laid back in her chair, arms crossed over her 'ample' bosom.

Suzanne stepped forward, "What do you mean, 'in charge of missing girls'? What do the police do about it? And just how many young girls are you talking about?"

The gypsy's eyes flashed and she put a sign up on her desk, saying she would return in twenty minutes. "I'm on break right now. Go see Andre!"

They stared at one another.

"This beats all," Steve said. "I don't trust that woman as far as I could throw her."

Suzanne put her arms around Susie and muttered, "As Rainey would say, don't that starch your shorts! Now what?"

Steve ran a hand through his hair and watched a tear roll down his niece's cheek. Checking his watch, he motioned them through the front door and out to the car. "Let's go see this Andre person, and then we'll get lunch somewhere.

Restaurants, bars and honky tonks stay open nearly around the clock in the French Quarter, except on Fat Tuesday, the end of Mardi Gras. At that time everything shutters down at midnight—no exceptions.

On this day, the festival was ongoing. As the three of them waded through the tourists, they found their way to Bourbon Street and Pat O'Brien's. It was full of revelers. An attractive woman sat at the piano, entertaining the crowd with her risqué songs and patter.

A cheeky waitress approached their table and asked to take their order.

"We don't want to order," Steve told her. "We're looking for Andre. He here?"

The waitress, whose name tag said she was Kathy, gave him a scowl. "Look, mister, we're in the food, drinks, and entertainment venue. No order, go somewhere else, okay?"

She turned to walk away, when Steve caught her arm. "Andre, is he here?"

Kathy jerked her arm away and started once again to leave. She spoke over her shoulder to them. "He works here at night, during the day, he works the front door at Preservation Hall."

After getting directions to the Hall, the trio made their way to the most famous blues venue in Louisiana. Not finding anyone at the door, they took seats and listened to the combo as they performed.

A few minutes later, they saw a tall, slender man exit the restroom. He wore a tuxedo with his hair slicked back. His smooth skin was the color of walnuts. He looked at the group, noticed Susie, turned and left by the back door.

11

Steve saw the hasty exit and followed. Out in the back alley, he looked in every direction but failed to see him. He returned to Suzanne and his niece.

"Well?"

"He got away. Obviously he saw us and, for whatever reason, he ran. He must know something. Maybe he recognized Cassie in Susie's face. We need to find him,

"But how, Uncle Steve, with all these people around? How in the world can we find him?" She began to cry softly. Suzanne put her arms around the girl for comfort.

"Let's get out of here, go get some lunch and regroup."

They found themselves in one of the more secluded cafes in town, where they ordered lunch.

Susie pushed her food around and finally put her napkin on top of her plate. "I guess I'm not very hungry. "I just want my sister back."

Steve grabbed her hand. "I understand, hon, but you need to keep up your strength. Eat a little. C'mon, try."

Chapter 3

The man they called the "Professor" spun around in his chair and gave a steely look to the tall man. "You're telling me there has been another death? This is totally unacceptable, Andre, these people are of no use to us dead." He got up and began to pace the room back and forth, back and forth. "What excuse do you have this time, idiot?"

Andre shifted uneasily on his chair. "Too much fentanyl, I reckon. How the hell do I know? I wasn't there, Professor. The others who are involved did it, not me."

"Don't snivel, you dumb bastard. It doesn't become you." He began to pace again, finally falling into his chair opposite Andre. "Where is the body?"

"Where I put the first one, in the cabin."

The professor rubbed his chin. "Okay, go back to work and I'll go out there tonight and get rid of it", he scowled at the tall creole. "This is your last mistake, do you understand, the very last. Tell those simpletons you recruited to work with you that no more will be tolerated. There will be consequences. Do you understand me, Andre?"

Andre nodded and made a quick exit. He was not about to tell the Professor about seeing the girl with her family. He was certain he had given her enough drugs to knock her out, but looking at her was like seeing a ghost. He had no idea how she could have gotten away. And he was grateful he left the Hall before she recognized him. More consequences from the Professor, he thought.

Andre returned to Preservation Hall, only to find out he had been fired for leaving his post without a word to anyone. Leaving the Hall, he walked to Pat O'Brien's to see if he could work dayshift there in addition to night.

The Thomases and Andre arrived at about the same time. Susie saw the man before he glimpsed her and shouted out to him. She grabbed Steve by the sleeve. "That's him, Uncle Steve, Andre. He was here the night Cassie disappeared!"

Springing into action, Steve lunged at the man just as Andre recognized the three of them and stepped back away from Steve. Turning, he ran into the crowd, with the three Thomases running after him. They dodged tourists, running zig zag through the crowds. Suzanne was hit in the face by someone tossing beads, but they kept on. At one time, Steve had almost reached the tall creole, but Andre slipped away, dodging into another restaurant and out the back door.

The three of them stood, panting, outside on the sidewalk as tourists stepped around them. Finally Steve caught his breath. Hugging his niece, he told her, "We'll get him, Susie. Not today, but we'll get him. Let's go back to the hotel and regroup, plan our strategy and catch our breath."

Walking into the lobby of the Hilton, Steve was handed a message from Chief Rochambeau.

"What's it say?" Suzanne asked.

14

Wadding the paper up, he angrily frowned at the two women. "Nothing. He says they are working on Cassie's case and hope to have some news in a few days."

"A few days?" Susie wailed.

"C'mon, let's catch the elevator." They disappeared behind the closing doors.

Chapter 4

It was midnight, and Suzanne and Susie were sleeping soundly. As quietly as he could, Steve slipped from bed, put on a pair of jeans and some loafers. Leaving the room, he walked silently down to the elevator and pushed the button for the basement.

The basement was dimly lit, with boxes and cartons stored on stacked shelves. Spare furniture was covered in plastic and stored on risers that took up a large portion of the space.

He looked around seeing nor hearing nothing, so he walked toward an exit door at the back of the warehouse like area. As he reached the door, he saw a shadow cross his path.

"Don't turn around," directed a disjointed voice. "Stay where you are and listen carefully."

Steve nodded, "Go on."

The man cleared his throat, "The man they call the Professor works at LSU, in the Science department. You need to talk to him about your niece."

"LSU, you say? How do I get there?" Steve asked but got no response.

Waiting only seconds, he turned around and saw that no one was there. The strange voice was gone, he listened for footsteps but heard none. He made a quick, perfunctory search of the basement but saw nothing and no sign that anyone had been there.

He slowly made his way back to the elevator and their room upstairs. Closing and locking the door behind him, he turned to find his wife staring at him.

"I found the note, Steve. That wasn't the police chief you met, was it?" she whispered.

Putting a finger to his lips, he nodded toward the bathroom, where they sat down and spoke softly in the darkness.

"Never saw who it was, Hon. Only heard a voice telling me not to turn around. I have no idea who it was or where the man got to. When I asked him something, he was gone. We need to go to see someone called the Professor at LSU tomorrow."

"The Professor? At a big university? That could be anyone."

"I know. And I don't think we should take Susie. She's too involved and too emotional right now. I don't even want to take you. It might be dangerous. I guess that's out of the question, isn't it?" In the darkness, he was unable to see the small smile on her face.

She reached out, and found his face, kissing him gently. "Don't even think it. We're a team, remember? What are we going to tell her when she says she wants to go along?"

"I have no idea. I'm hoping something will come to me at breakfast"

***

Morning seemed to come too early for the three of them, Susie again pushing her food around. Her aunt and uncle sat quietly as they contemplated what they would say to her.

Finally, Steve took his niece's hand and spoke quietly to her. "Susie, Suzanne and I are going to talk to someone today who may help us find Casie. We're only going to talk to him, nothing more. I think it would be best if you stayed here and waited for us. You can rest and we'll tell you everything that's said when we return. We won't be long."

Susie left the dining room in tears, mumbling about being treated like a baby.

Steve sighed in exasperation, "Well, that went well didn't it?

He grabbed the check and his wife's hand, and got up from the table. "C'mon. Lets go to LSU. The sooner we go, the sooner we can get back."

Chapter 5

"How far is it?" Suzanne asked.

"The hotels' concierge told me about 40 miles to Baton Rouge. It shouldn't take us long to get there."

"I still think," she added, "we're looking for a needle in a haystack, trying to find someone called Professor on a huge college campus. Everyone there must be called professor."

"I know," Steve sighed. "But it's the only clue we have, and this Andre person seems to have disappeared into thin air. Every time I check in with Rochambeau, he tells me they are working on it and, no, they have not found her. I doubt he's even looking, quite frankly. I hope to find her first and get her home."

"Cassie and Gene still do not know?"

"I'll tell them the whole story once we find their daughter, once I know they won't have to worry."

Riding in silence for several miles, they finally spied the university, the huge stadium a standout in the area. Driving until they found the front entrance, Steve pulled in front of the administration building.

The office was located just inside the front door, to the right. It was one of many offices located along the lengthy hall, each one marked by a wrought iron sign over the door telling visitors what was inside.

The couple approached the secretary, whose name tag said she was Mrs. Evans. Steve explained the situation to her and wondered if she knew of a person on campus known as the Professor.

"Really, Mr. Thomas, all our teaching personnel go by the moniker Professor. And," she added rather indignantly, "I can tell you now, that none of them would be involved in kidnapping, sir. We have only the most reputable and impeccable people working here."

"I'm sure of that, Mrs. Evans. But I have it on good authority that this professor person is involved with the university." He then asked to speak to the chancellor.

Mabel Evans shook her head. "I'm sorry, he is not available. Anything else I can help you with today?"

Shaking his head no, he turned, took his wife's arm and had started for the door when Suzanne spoke up. "Is there, perhaps, an employee of some kind who might go by the nickname of the professor?"

Mabel again shook her head and went back to her typing. Just as the Thomases got to the door, she hollered out, "Wait! In the mechanical building, you know, where all the furnaces and boilers are located? Our superintendent of maintenance is sometimes called The Professor by the students. But, again, I can vouch for him."

Getting directions to the mechnical building, Steve and Suzanne got back in the car and headed that way.

***

The man everyone called the Professor, put down his phone and stared at the old man sitting across from him. "Old man," he began, "I've been told they are on their way here. Sit behind this desk and do what I told you to do and say what I told you to say, kapish? Once they leave, you can go to the doctor. Got it?"

"And if I don't?" he wheezed

The professor leaned across the desk and was almost touching faces with the old man. "You'll die, one reason being you will be off 'the list'. Do we understand one another?"

The old man nodded, while taking the chair behind the desk. His companion stepped into the closet and shut the door, while they waited on Steve and Suzanne.

***

After mutual introductions and some small talk, Steve got to the point, recounting the abduction of Cassie and the lack of progress so far.

"So, they call you the professor?"

The old man shrugged and peered over his glasses at them. "Kids. They got a name for everyone," he chuckled.

"How long you been with the university," they asked him.

"Near unto 60 years."

"Aren't you a little old to be messing with all this machinery and things? Aren't you afraid of getting hurt at your age?" Steve wondered.

21

Again the old man shrugged, and briefly told them that occasionally one of the engineering students came over and loaned a hand. "What can I do for you ?" he wheezed.

Steve moved a little closer to the desk while he looked in the old fella's eyes. "Do you know anything about a missing young woman, 21, happened couple days ago. She was kidnapped from the French Quarter."

"Awful, the things that go on nowadays. I haven't been to the French Quarter in years, tell me," he leaned in closer, "is Pat O'Brien's still there, on the bayou?"

"Yes, it is." Steve stood up and motioned for Suzanne and him to leave, "Thanks for your time, Old Fella, sorry to bother you. Don't work too hard now, hear?"

As he and Suzanne were driving back to New Orleans, The Professor was headed for the big bayou. He had a job to do, and one of Andres messes to clean up.

Chapter 6

The 'professor' pulled his canoe over to the muddy shore. He got out, put on rubber gloves and walked to the cabin, which wasn't more than a shack at this point. Windows were broken. What passed as a floor was warped and spotted with bleached out water stains. The odor of green algae and death co-mingled, making the man slightly nauseated as he went to work, sealing up a bag that held the corpse.

Struggling to throw it over his shoulder, he slowly made his way to the door. Laying it as best as he could, he placed the body bag on the bottom of the canoe, where it tipped the boat precariously.

He paddled slowly further into the bayou, the occasional alligator eyeing him from the shore where they sunned themselves.

Once the man reached the deepest part of the bayou—almost to the open waters of the gulf—he threw it overboard, watched it sink, then paddled back to the cabin. He beached the canoe and walked thru all the thick, weedy underbrush to the place where he had left the pickup. Plowing thru underbrush and mossy ground, eventually he came out onto the road, where he made a hasty retreat back to Baton Rouge, convinced that no one saw him. He felt confident nothing could be traced back to him and knew full well that Andre and his small crew would bear the burden of guilt over the entire operation.

He was wrong. He had been seen and his activities were noted. And written down.

***

Steve, his wife and niece sat in the mezzanine bar of the Hilton, nursing drinks. Suzanne was especially pensive as she stared off into space, Susie was downcast, and Steve was beside himself with frustration

He reached over and touched his wife's arm, "What is it, hon? What has you so thoughtful?"

She smiled at him before she spoke. "I was just thinking. We've talked with two people so far that have mentioned the bayou to us. That last guy—the maintenance guy—made a point to mention the bayou to us. Maybe we ought to check it out?"

"Yeah, I was thinking the same thing. But New Orleans is surrounded by bayous. Where do we start and how do we go about it? Either one of you have any ideas?"

Susie put her Coke down and looked from one to the other, "I think Andre is the key. We need to find him, and soon. I want my sister back," she cried.

Steve patted her on the arm. "We'll get her back. Don't you worry. In the meantime, we need to keep looking for Andre. As my brilliant niece pointed out, he is the key." He pulled out his phone and began dialing.

"Who're you calling, Uncle Steve?"

"Rochambeau's office. I want to make sure we keep checking in, so he'll know we're serious about this, and just maybe, he'll get on the stick with this thing. From what little we've heard, I gather there are other kidnappings going on.

"Now look," he went on, "we have to eat. So let's go up to the room, change and go get dinner somewhere and plan our next step."

"Susie," he said, "I want you to officially checkout of your hotel and move in with us while we do this searching. We have room and I'd feel better having you close by. That okay?"

"Yes, absolutely," the girl enthused. "I may as well, especially since I spent last night with you anyway, and all day."

Steve got up from the small table, nodded at Suzanne and said further, "Good. I'll go clear it with the front desk and meet you both back in the room in about forty-five minutes."

Susie excused herself also and walked to the elevator that would take her to the lobby floor.

Suzanne watched them both leave, sighed and sought out their waiter to ask him some questions about this Andre that everybody seemed to know but couldn't or wouldn't pinpoint his location.

None of the three wanted the others to see how worried they were. After speaking with him, she too left, heading up to their room.

Chapter 7

Susie, exhausted by the stress, went to bed early, while Steve and Suzanne sat on the couch in the small sitting area. They were planning their activities for the next day when the phone in the room rang a short buzzing sound. Steve grabbed for it before it could wake his niece.

"Meet me in front of the fountain that's in front of the big cathedral at midnight. Don't bring anyone with you", a muffled voice instructed him, before he hung up.

After he hung up, Steve turned to his wife,

"Who was that?' she asked

Steve shook his head. "Don't know. He didn't say. A muffled voice told me to come alone to the St. Louis Cathedral at midnight tonight. I have no idea who it was."

"Surely you're not going—alone yet—at midnight."

"This person obviously knows us and what we' re doing, so how can I not go? It might be something that will help us find Cassie."

"But alone? Dear, it's too dangerous. We should go together. Two is much better than one. I'll put on some dark clothes and stay in the shadows. I will not be seen. Please, Steve. This is important to me. I want to be sure you're all right."

Running a hand through his hair, Steve shook his head. "I don't know, Suze. It might be dangerous." He saw the pleading look on her face and stared back at her.

"All the more reason to have me along. I'll take my cell phone and if you get into trouble I'll dial for help and scream really loud." She gave him a weak smile.

Steve paced the room slowly, looked at his wife, and paced some more. Finally he sat down next to her. "All right, but stay out of sight and don't make a sound. Hear?"

She pretended to lock her lips sealed, and went in search of some dark clothing to wear to the rendezvous.

***

Back in Beryl's Cove, Skank sat straight up in bed and rubbed his chest. The motion roused Rainey and she rolled over and opened one eye to peer at her husband. Elvis had been sleeping on their bed. He stirred when they did and jumped down, going in search of Dawg, so he could cuddle up with him.

"What is it ?" she asked.

Skank thumped his chest. "That feeling here. Someone's in danger. I can feel it."

"Is it Steve or Suzanne? They're out in Kentucky, watching some races. Maybe we should call them, you know, just to see, and let them know the pets are okay?"

"It's almost midnight, Rainey. I don't know, maybe we could. Let me ponder on it a little while."

***

It was midnight, straight up, and Steve sat on a bench in front of the St. Louis fountain. He looked all around,

27

trying to see if someone was there also. A few stragglers walked by but, for the most part, all the action was back in the French Quarter.

Suddenly a man dressed all in black, his face obscured by a hat, walked swiftly toward him. Hurrying passed, he dropped a piece of paper into Steve's lap and—as quickly as he could—went behind him. Steve was stuffing the paper into his pocket when instantly a chloroform cloth covered his face.

Suzanne watched in horror from the shadows. She was about to show herself by emerging from the trees, but at that moment her cell phone rang. She didn't have time to do anything. As she fumbled with the phone, chloroform overcame her and she slumped to the ground.

***

Steve was the first to wake up. He rubbed his face and hair and glanced over at his wife, who was still asleep on the floor. The only illumination coming from the full moon that cast a dim light into the interior of the place.

He fished around for his cell phone. He wanted to call the hotel and speak to Susie, to let her know they were all right, but his phone was gone, His wallet was still there, with everything in it. Finding the slip of paper that was dropped in his lap, he unfolded it and tried to read it.

As Suzanne began to wake up and stir, he went over to the window frame and read it by moonlight: "You were told to come alone to the church. Disobey orders again and you'll never get your niece back. Take the jon boat that's outside and go deeper into the bayou. You'll find what you're looking for."

There was no signature. By this time Suzanne was awake. She groggily asked him where they were and what happened.

"I think we were drugged," he answered. "And from the looks of things outside, we're stranded in the bayou somewhere. Here," he stretched out his hand, "let me help you up."

"What time is it anyway?" She was wobbly on her feet. Holding her head, she complained of a headache.

"It's 4 am," he said, gazing at his watch. "You okay?"

She stood up and looked around at her surroundings.

"Susie? My cell phone's been taken, yours?"

She felt her pockets and shook her head. "Gone. Now what?"

Steve handed her the note he had been given, told her they should head for the boat and try to find Cassie. "We don't have any other choice," he told her, as they left the cabin.

"Boy, this is one for that book you're supposed to be writing," she told him.

***

Skank Peterson was waiting on Chief Sowinski when Nathan came in for work that morning.

"Skank, what in the world?"

"I got this feeling, here," he thumped his chest. "And I ain't never wrong, Chief. I think Steve and Suzanne are in trouble. Rainey tried to call Susanne last night on her cell and there was no answer. Didn't even go to voicemail. We're worried."

Nathan hunched his shoulders and opened his hands in a questioning mode. "So?"

"You don't understand, Chief. Suzanne never shuts off her cell. We communicate a lot and she calls often to check on the pets. Somethin's wrong, I tell you." He thumped his chest again.

Sowinski eyed Skank, the man seemed genuinely concerned. "Skank," he began. "I don't honestly know what I can do about this. They still in Kentucky?"

"Far as I know," was the reply.

After Skank left, Nathan sat there a while, thinking. Knowing that the old swam rat was nearly always right about these things, he picked up the phone and asked Genevieve to get him the police chief in Louisville, Kentucky.

Chapter 8

Steve paddled the sturdy jon boat deeper into the bayou. Moss hung from trees, patting them gently on the face as they went. Occasionally, an alligator or large turtle would poke its head out of the water to give them a blank stare. A large bird flew at them, making a loud cry as it did so. Suzanne admitted to being a little bit frightened by it all.

They passed some very shabby cabins, some not more than lean-tos, as they went. They watched as a large gator surfaced and grabbed a nearby waterfowl, submerging again as they paddled past. Suzanne shivered at the sight.

"What are we looking for?" she whispered.

"Don't rightly know, but I'll know it when I see it," he replied.

Eventually they came upon another cabin that seemed empty except for the small boat and motor tied to a broken pier. Steve pulled in alongside of it and helped his wife up onto the soggy shore.

As they entered they were assailed by the strong odor of disinfectant and noticed all the ropes and chains down one side of the large room. Suzanne put her hand over her mouth. A look of terror crossed her face when she realized Cassie had probably been hidden here. Tears welled up in her eyes.

They walked every inch of the room, noticing an occasional spot of dried blood. As they turned around, two men watching them moved forward.

"I'm Andre," the tall creole said. "And this," he pointed to a smaller man, a genuine albino with snow white hair, pale eyes and milk white skin, "this is the 'Professor.'"

The albino stepped forward and held out a limp hand to Steve. "I believe you're looking for me, Mr. Thomas." He gave them a sneer. "Welcome to you both." He half bowed to Suzanne.

Andre left the room, only to return with two wooden chairs that he placed before the Professor. "Won't you have a seat?"

***

They had been tied to their chairs, blindfolded and gagged, but not before being shown another room in the cabin that contained a hospital bed, an IV stand and some medical monitors. No explanation—just being told that the albino and Andre would return later that night and start the "proceedings" on them.

Steve rocked his chair back and forth in an attempt to dislodge the ropes binding his arms and hands. He guessed, from the sounds he heard, that Suzanne was trying the same thing.

She had worked her gag loose and was now able to speak. "I'm going to try and 'dance' my chair over to you, Steve. Maybe we can somehow untie each other.

I'm still blindfolded. So keep talking and I'll try to aim toward your voice.

Steve began reciting the alphabet while his wife did her best to scoot toward him. Her effort took some time, with Suzanne resting every so often. Finally she reached him and then began maneuvering her chair to where their tied hands met.

Struggling with the ropes, they heard the door open. They were met with the smell of the bayou. and hot, musty air.

He gave a start when his blindfold was taken off and he looked up into the eyes of Officer Grace Delaney. Standing with her was the woman they knew as Mother Rosalie.

"What the—"

Grace spoke as she freed Suzanne. "Sorry for the deception, Mr. Thomas. Rosalie and I are working undercover to help the chief bust up this ring of organ harvesters we've got going on in New Orleans." She was rubbing Suzannes wrists, helping to get the circulation going.

"We followed Andre and the Professor out here, staying clear until they were well out of the area. Then we looked around for a while."

"Looking for what?" Steve interrupted, rubbing his own wrists and ankles. "I sure wish you would have told us all this."

"We couldn't blow our cover," Mother Rosalie told him. She was helping Suzann to stand up.

"All right, talk. What's this organ harvesting all about? And we still haven't found my niece."

"Well," Grace began, "there are folks who are willing to pay extremely high prices for the organs, like kidneys or partial livers. Even lungs and, in some cases, hearts. Andre and the Professor front a ring of people who go in search of healthy people, like your niece, whose body parts are healthy. They do the kidnapping and then transplant the good organ into the waiting patient. It's all done without waiting on some kind of waiting list that often takes years to get the organ. It's a very lucrative operation they have going. Also extremely illegal and, quite often, accidents happen and the donor dies."

Suzanne shivered, "how ghoulish."

"My niece?" Steve asked them.

"We're not sure. Andre and the Professor, when we find them, will spend many years in prison for this. As for Cassie, I have an idea. We've got a boat tied up outside. Come along and we'll follow my hunch."

Chapter 9

After leaving the big bayou, Officer Delaney and Mother Rosalie left in an unmarked police vehicle. The Thomas couple followed in their rental as they headed back to Baton Rouge. An hour later, they pulled up to the checkpoint at LSU. Grace flashed her badge for them to be admitted and drove around the back side of the campus to the mechanical building.

It was still early. Most of the students and faculty had not yet stirred or begun classes. As they all got out, Steve approached the officer.

"Suzanne and I have already been here, Grace. The old man who is the maintenance guy is a dead end."

"'Old man maintenance guy'? No such thing, Mr. Thomas. Their chief maintenance engineer is the albino everyone calls the Professor. His name is Carl Tarkington, and we've been after him and his band of ghouls for many months now."

"Well," he began, "if you know all this about him— even where he works—why isn't he in jail, all of them?"

"We can't catch them, that's why", she said irritably. "Every time we get close, they move their operation, kit and kaboodle, somewhere else and, of course, we want their victims also, but they too seem to have disappeared."

"So, why are we here now?"

"Because, when they discover that you and the missus are gone, they are going to want to come back here and move their junk again. We'll wait for them. In the meantime, I'm moving my cruiser out of sight and I suggest you do the same with your car. We don't want to tip them off before we can catch them."

The four of them secured the automobiles and found safe, discreet hiding places in and around the office and business door. Slowly the campus came alive while the group waited. Eventually Steve and Suzanne saw the old man they had mistaken for the "Professor." He was pushing a large broom back and forth along the floor.

Suddenly the door opened. Tarkington and Andre entered the room, turned on the light and went to the computer. From opposite sides of the office, Steve and Officer Delaney slowly edged their way across the floor toward them.

In a split-second Andre looked up, saw Steve nearing and bolted for the door. Steve followed, but Andre had youth and speed in his favor as he wove his way around engineering students, janitorial employees and boxes of supplies. Steve chased as well as he could. Following him to the basement, he found himself staring down a long hall with doors and nooks lining the wall. He bent over, hands on knees, and drew in big breaths, trying to stop the pounding his heart was making.

Unable to catch Andre, he went outside by the nearest door and found his three cohorts standing over a cruiser door while they put a handcuffed Tarkington in the back seat.

Suzanne rushed to her husband. "He told us where Cassie is." She was excited. "Let's go get her and head home. I've had quite enough excitement for one vacation,"

Still panting, Steve looked at his wife and slowly shook his head. "No. I want this bastard. We'll get Cassie, then I'm going after him."

Chapter 10

They left Grace and Mother Rosalie and on Suzanne's instructions, headed back to the French Quarter. Officer Delaney had told them that, as soon as Tarkington was booked, they would meet up with them at the house to which they were now going.

Even in broad daylight, sections of the city of New Orlean were in shadow, hidden from view by many trees and high shrubs. Most of the homes on the outskirts were shrouded in dark shadows. It was to one of these houses that Steve and Suzanne were headed. It was in the garden district, where fine and palatial homes were in abundance—lush gardens and courtyards ringed in ornate wrought iron fences.

They sat in the car, looking out at the surroundings.

"Looks very upper crust to me, doncha think?" Suzanne addressed her husband. "Doesn't look like anything illegal and nefarious could be taking place in that house. I mean, wow, look at it!" she exclaimed.

"I'm going to drive around the back and see if there is an alleyway I can park in. I'd just would prefer not to be seen, especially if we have to kidnap her back."

Driving behind the house, they saw walled gardens, bricked courtyards and, occasionally, small vegetable or flower plots and ornate benches. They found a shady spot a block away. They parked the car, locked and headed toward their destination.

Still early enough, the hoi polloi were not stirring around. Probably waiting on high tea, Steve chuckled to himself.

They slipped easily into the backyard, stuck to as many shadows as they could, and approached what looked like a basement door: one of the old timey ones, with slanted, outside locking doors, that opened upwards. Steve quickly picked the lock and opened the door enough for himself and Suzann to slide through.

The basement was pitch black, not unlike the one back in Beryl's Cove when he and Suzanne were searching for a murderer in the old Murdoch house.

He took a small penlight in his pocket, turned it on and scanned the room with it. Laundry appliances, basket and clothes chute were the first things he saw. In the corner was a pool table covered in plastic and an anteroom holding a ping pong table.

"Looks like recreation heaven," Suzanne whispered to him.

Along one wall, close to the washer and dryer, was an old double sink and faucet with sprayer.

Suddenly they heard the door to upstairs open and a middle aged woman walked to the clothes chute, gathered the dirty clothes and proceeded to fill the washing machine. She left the same way she entered, turning out the light as she did so. They heard muffled conversation from upstairs. Then the speakers moved away and all was quiet and dark once again as Steve and Suzanne emerged from behind a giant heating furnace.

"What now?" she asked.

"Probably the help. Let's wait a few minutes and see if they leave the house."

Twenty minutes later the woman returned, put the washing in the dryer and called upstairs, "You ready? I've got the clothes on dry and I want to get back before they get back from breakfast."

"Where we goin'?" A male voice answered her.

"Need a few things from the market. Shouldn't take us long," was the reply.

"I'll get the car."

The Thomases gazed out a small crack in the outside door just in time to see an older man in a chauffeur's cap, pull a Mercedes around to the back door. The woman got in and they drove off.

Steve motioned for his wife and they went up the steps to the main floor and opened the door.

Laying in front of the basement door was a large German Shepherd dog, who immediately sat up and began to growl at the intruders. Suzanne saw that they were in some kind of breakfast room, the kitchen refrigerator just steps away. While the dog held Steve at bay, she slipped behind him to the refrigerator. Opening it, she saw a pack of lunchmeat. Taking two slices from the package, she threw them to the dog, who was distracted by his treat allowing them to sneak past and have a quick look around.

"As my friend Gregg used to say," Steve muttered, "the rich, they are different. Bedrooms must be upstairs. Let's go."

Going bedroom to bedroom, at the fifth room they found Cassie asleep—obviously drugged—with an IV drip in her arm.

They acted quickly. Steve pulled out the IV, picked up his niece and headed for the stairs. Entering the living room, they were met by the obvious owners, the man pointing a gun at them.

"I suggest you take that young lady back upstairs where you found her. She's our daughter, gravely ill. Now take her back and get the hell out of my home!" he shouted.

Standing there, Cassie slung over his shoulder, Steve stared the man down. "She's most assuredly not your daughter. She's our niece, drugged of course, and I'd like to know what the hell you're doing with her."

At that moment Officer Delaney and Mother Rosalie entered the home. Grace Delaney with her service revolver pointed at the man and woman who were holding a gun on the Thomases.

"Well if it isn't Mr. and Mrs. Van Dam. I might've known you'd be involved in this, Van Dam. Mind telling me, after you hand over that gun, just what is going on here?"

Claud Van Dam put down the gun, gave a defeated smile to his wife, coughed a bit, and told the group— now joined by Chief Rochambeau—what the plan was. The dog, Rocky, having been tasered, lay whimpering on the kitchen floor.

"That young woman was to be my life saver," he began. "She was scheduled to donate a lung to me tomorrow. I have emphysema, very bad. I gave good money to Andre to find me a healthy donor so I can live, dammit. I'm an important member of this community, a scion of business. Surely my life is worth her sacrifice." He gave them a defiant look.

Incensed, Steve lunged at the man, only to be held back by the chief. "What about Cassie's life?" he screamed at the man. "What about her life?"

Van Dam shrugged. "She's young. Her recuperative ability is vastly better than mine and I'm needed. What's she ever done, anyway?" He coughed again, this time more violently.

Steve lunged at the man once more and, again, was held back by the police chief.

"And, the deaths?" Rochambeau asked.

Van Dam shook his head. "That was unfortunate, but certainly not my fault. We—myself, wife and servants—were giving her the best care, and she would have received the finest hospital care after her surgery, I can assure you."

"And then what?" Rochambeau inquired, as he put cuffs on the Van Dams.

Van Dam just shrugged.

The officer accompanying the chief ran into the room and said the servants were returning.

Rochambeau grinned and said, "Cuff 'em, and book 'em on accessory to murder and kidnapping. Take the hound," he nodded to the dog who had slunk into the room, "to the pound."

The chief turned to Steve and Suzanne. "If you think she needs medical attention," he pointed to Cassie," take her to the hospital and tell them to bill the city of New

Orleans. I am truly sorry for all this, Mr. Thomas, truly sorry. Eventually we'll get Andre and his band of ghouls, but in the meantime, after the girl has recovered, I suggest you all return to North Carolin and maybe visit our city under happier circumstances. We'll need the girl's testimony at some point, you understand."

Steve carried Cassie to their rental car and, laying her on the back seat, he slid behind the wheel. The chief tipped his hat to them as they drove away.

They drove in silence for several minutes, then Suzanne spoke up. "Steve?"

His jaw set, he turned to his wife and told her, "I have unfinished business. I'm taking you both back to the hotel, and I'll see you when my business is done."

Nothing more was said. Suzanne just nodded, as they drove on in silence.

Chapter 11

Cassie had been put to bed in their room, her sister hovering close. Taking the IV out of her arm stopped the flow of anesthetic, but she was slow in waking up. Occasionally, she would make a sound or move in her sleep, but, she was soundly out of it.

Suzanne left the girl to answer a knock at the door. She opened it enough to peep out and saw her brother-in-law and sister-in-law standing there in a rage. They almost fell into the room as soon as the door was opened. Gene was beside himself. "Why weren't we told about this and where is our daughter?"

Suzanne pointed to the bedroom area, where Suzie was lying next to her twin, holding her hand. "Mama, Daddy," she cried, "Don't be mad. Uncle Steve and Aunt Suzanne saved her life. It was my idea not to tell you at the beginning."

"You'd better explain yourself little girl," her mother hissed.

After checking on the girl, making sure their daughter was okay, Gene and Cassie, followed by Suzanne and Suzie, went into the sitting area. Suzanne ordered coffee all around from room service. Suzie began the story, all about how they decided to check out New Orleans and Mardi Gras, the kidnapping and her text to her aunt and uncle, and about how they had come to their rescue, finally finding Cassie.

Tarkington was taken to jail, and bonded out almost immediately, disappearing once again.

When Suzie was finished, Suzanne asked Gene how they had found them.

"It all began with Skank", he said.

"Skank?"

"You know how he gets the feelings, inside," Gene thumped his chest. "Well, he was thumping away, went to see Nathan, who believed him. They checked with the Police Chief of Louisville, who did some digging and found out where you were staying. He called the hotel, only to be told you had checked out and were headed for New Orleans. Sooo, Nathan called the police chief here and got the full story. He informed us you were at the Hilton. And here we are."

Cassie moaned and stirred a little, causing her mother to run to the bedroom and kneel at her side. Taking the girl's hand, Mother Cassie cooed softly to her as Gene and Suzie joined her at bedside.

After a few moments alone with his family, Gene went to Suzanne and sat beside her. "We'll talk later. Where's Steve?"

"He went after this Andre person, but I don't know where he is Gene. He could be anywhere in the French Quarter."

Her brother-in-law nodded and headed for the door. He left as suddenly as he arrived.

Suzanne gave Cassie a shrug. "May as well settle in, ladies. This could take some time."

Chapter 12

Making sure all three women were locked in and secure, Gene left, hoping to catch up with his brother, and continue the search for Andre.

Steve was walking the streets of the French Quarter, dodging revelers as he went. One man stood at the corner he had just left, naked with a Hawaiian flower lei around his neck. Some of the women were parading bare breasted through the streets.

He stopped at every restaurant and asked about Andre. They all knew of him, but said he was a 'floater' who went wherever he could work. No one knew where he lived.

Gene had not picked up his brother's trail, though he got the same answers everywhere he inquired.

Both men stopped in at Cafe du Monde for coffee and beignets, before continuing their search. Still, their paths did not cross and the large tourist crowd was hampering their search.

***

Out on the bayou, Andre slowly motored toward the cabin. The word had spread of the arrest of the Van Dam couple and their servants. He and the Professor agreed to meet at the cabin and plan their next move.

Andre glided his jon boat in beside the Professor's and, tying up, he entered the cabin.

The albino sat on a chair facing the door and, when Andre entered, he jumped the man, attempting to strangle him. Andre pushed him off, knocking him to the floor, where he kicked him to the wall.

"Get off me, you piece of shit. Don't put your hands on me. This whole operation is falling apart, thanks to you, 'professor.' You got greedy. you piece of slime, and now we got four people under arrest and men out there chasing me. And I'm not going down alone, you creep!" He kicked the man again, causing him to double over in pain

"You're nothing but a stupid janitor!" Andre screamed. He looked around the room and seeing nothing but the chair, he picked it up and smashed it over his victim's head. The albino was dead.

Andre made his way through the swampy waters of the bayou and, upon reaching a certain point, dumped the body overboard, weighted, and tied up. It would sink to the bottom with the rest of his "mistakes' and, hopefully, the alligators would feed on all of them.

***

Gene walked for what he felt was hours, resting every so often on park benches. It was getting dark. When he looked up the street, he saw him, his brother chasing after a man who dodged people, balloons, party debris and drunks laid out on the street. It had to be Andre, he reasoned, and joined the chase. Steve was a block ahead of him but Gene pumped hard to catch up. He saw both men head down an alley between two restaurants and Gene followed.

Steve caught Andre by his shirt collar and pulled him to a stop, where he pushed him to the ground and began attacking the man. He pummeled him, kicked him in the groin and slapped the man's face several times. He pulled his arm back to hit Andre again when something caught it in midair. He looked up into the face of his brother and Geen pulled him off the creole.

"Don't do it bro. Don't make yourself another victim of his. He's done. Out cold. Let him live to face his fate," he said while he called 911.

Chapter 13

The two couples sat in Rochambeau's' office. They left Cassie and Suzie at the hotel to rest or go to the pool while they talked with the chief.

"Sit down, won't you?" He waved to the chairs around his office. "Tell me how the girl is doing, Mr. Thomas".

Gene and Steve glanced at one another. Finally Gene spoke up. "The twins are our daughters, Chief", he smiled at his wife. "They are both traumatized beyond belief. What kind of a city are you running here, Rochambeau? They both could have easily been killed!"

"I understand your distress, Mr.Thomas, and I apologize for what has happened."

"You apologize? That's it, an apology? And as for understanding my distress, I doubt you do, unless of course you have a daughter that was kidnapped, drugged for days on end and scheduled to have a kidney and possibly a lung surgically taken from her body!" Gene was shouting now. He took his wife's hand and refused to look the police chief in the eye. "Apology!"

Steve patted his brother on the shoulder, trying to calm him down.

Rochambeau gave a weak smile. "I certainly can't blame you for your anger and, rest assured, this band of organ thieves will never see the light of day. They

49

are also guilty of murder, including that of this 'professor,' who was the brains of the outfit. Andre and his gang merely carried out orders. We've been after them for quite some time but, like you, we had difficulty locating them all. They moved from place to place and were always on the move. New Orleans is a much safer city now, thanks to the four of you." He got up, and walked to his desk, using his intercom to call for his assistant to make coffee.

"Please forgive my bad manners. May I offer you some coffee?"

Gene shrugged him off and, with a final glare, grabbed his wife Cassie, and strode from the office. Steve stood up and shook Rochambeau's' hand, and left with Suzanne, following his brother and sister-in-law out to the car.

The chief watched at the window as they peeled out of the parking lot. Picking up the phone, he barked into it, "Cancel the coffee. Have the Van Dams been released yet?" he asked. "Good," he continued, "Tell them I want them in my office as soon as they can get here. We need to regroup."

Once the police chief hung up, Officer Grace Delaney silently hung up her extension. Shaking her head, she took her cell phone into the restroom and dialed Mother Rosalie. When the woman answered, Grace uttered very few words. "It's not over," she whispered into the receiver, turned and walked back to her desk.

***

Back at the hotel, the two couples found Cassie and Suzie playing card, Coca Colas on the table next to them.

"Get dressed and packed," their father ordered. "We're leaving—now! I want nothing more to do with this godforsaken city. NOW, I said!"

It was a forlorn group that left the hotel thirty minutes later. Steve and Suzanne walked them to their car. Waving goodbye, they walked arm in arm back inside.

Opting to stay by themselves, they ordered room service for their dinner and spent the night together— alone.

Part 2

Chapter 14

Deciding to return to Beryls Cove the fastest way possible, they flew into the Wilmington airport and took one of the outer banks shuttles to the ferry and across the water to the cove.

Dropping their luggage in the front hall, Suzanne phoned Rainey and asked her to bring the pets home at her convenience. Thirty minutes later the big redhead burst into the house, Elsie on a lead beside her and Dawg and Elvis trotting along behind.

"Girlfriend!" she screamed as she hugged her best friend, "we have been so worried about you! It was Skank, you know, who put the search in motion to find you. He's been thumping his chest ever since you left." She went from one to the other, hugging them. Dawg was jumping up and down as much as it was possible for him to jump and Elvis took his place in front of the sliding glass door of the sunroom in his usual place, seemingly oblivious to the commotion going on around him.

Steve hugged her back and told her how grateful they were for Skanks "feelings, in here" as he always said. "It saved our lives," he told her.

"Where is he anyway?" Steve asked her.

"He had a charter he took out earlier today, but I messaged him that you were back."

"He got anything lined up for tomorrow?"

"Not that I know of. Why?"

Steve smiled at his wife. "Tell him I'll be round early and he and I can spend the day fishing for ourselves for a change."

After Rainy left, they settled the pets in, unpacked and Suzanne fell across the bed, exhausted from the worry, and the trip.

Steve poked his head in the bedroom, "Gonna take a shower, Hon. Be right with you."

A big smile on her face, Suzanne laid there until she heard the water running and, stripping down, she joined her husband in the shower.

Chapter 15

Large Bear, who everyone knew was the biggest human being in the world, was on patrol. Years ago he had signed on as a part-time, volunteer deputy and he had done such a good job Chief Sowinski hired him on as a permanent member of his squad.

Chamois cloths covering the hooves of his massive horse, Large Bear rode through the streets of Beryls Cove silent as a mouse. This month he was on night duty and he knew full well that when he reported in the morning to turn in his report, early rising tourists would applaud as he rode through town thinking him to be some kind of special effect.

The citizens loved the big Indian. They felt secure with him patrolling their town. As he rode by he noticed the light still on at Maybelle Wilson's house and he pondered whether or not to knock on her door and call attention to it, maybe save her some money on her electric bill. He rode on and when he made rounds again in an hour, the light was still burning. He opted not to go to her door. "Probably fell asleep reading," he muttered to himself and continued to patrol.

Maybelle lived next door to Hortense Wilkerson, a distant cousin of Maybelle's deceased husband. The two women talked over the hedge every day, trading produce. And Hortense kept her neighbors supplied with fresh eggs from her chickens.

As usual, Hortens was up early, gathering eggs and feeding her chickens. Gathering an apron full of eggs, she crossed the yard into Maybelle's and knocked at the back door. No answer. So she knocked again. And when she still got no answer, she walked inside the unlocked door and put the eggs in the refrigerator. Noticing the recently baked cherry coffee cake, she put on a pot of coffee and went in search of her neighbor.

"Bet she's in that big soaking tub she ordered last year." she thought.

The cherry coffee cake was a recipe from the Brown twins. They gave them away on special occasions and, when they died, Suzanne Thomas got the recipe. Now, every woman in the Cove baked the delicacy.

Well, she found Maybelle in bed, dead. Not knowing for sure what to do next, she called Gladys Smith, her neighbor from the other side of her house, and Gladys came running over.

"Poor Maybelle," Gladys cried, forgetting for the moment that the woman was diabetic, had a heart condition and was 100 pounds overweight.

"At least we can have a cup of coffee while we figure out what to do next," Hortense offered. "Excuse me for a minute, Gladys," Hortense left the kitchen, went over to her house and ,once outside again, she fired her gun for good measure. Can't be too careful, she thought, just in case some nefarious trouble maker was lurking about and had had a hand in killing poor

Maybelle. She explained all this to Gladys when she returned to Maybelle's kitchen,

In the meantime, Gladys had phoned some of the other neighbors who were now gathering on the Wilson's front lawn in yard chairs having a round table discussion of the morning's events.

Gladys decided to serve that cherry coffee cake to everyone, since poor Maybelle wouldn't be eating it.

Large Bear had returned to the police station and was about to go inside when he noticed the group across the street, having what looked like a picnic. He found the chief engrossed in paperwork.

"What's going on over at the Wilson's place?" he asked, while taking a chair in front of Nathan's desk.

"Huh?"

"Turn around, Chief and see what's outside your window. The whole neighborhood is having a picnic over there, I think. I went by her place last night and She had a light burning the entire time."

Grabbing his cap, Nathan pulled Large Bear along. "Let's go see."

Once on the lawn across the street, the two men were offered a cup of coffee and a sliver of coffee cake.

"What's going on?" He asked, sipping the heavenly brew. "Where's Maybelle?"

"Dead," were the collective voices.

"What do you mean 'dead'?" Nathan was incredulous

Hortense scowled at the lawmen. "For Pete's sake, Nathan. Dead as in not breathing!"

Nathan stood up, knocking over the lawn chair someone had pushed towards him. "You mean the woman is inside dead and you all are out here having a picnic?"

Hortense was beside herself now. "Not a picnic, Chief. We're here discussing what to do next and the coffee cake will do Maybelle no good now. So we're eating it. Helps us to think!"

Nathan nodded to Large Bear. "Go find her, deputy, while I deal with this bunch."

"Land sakes, Chief, I just told you she was dead—in her bed. Peaceful as a babe."

Nathan threw his cap down on the ground and cast an evil eye at Hortense. "Woman," he exclaimed, "I am this far from putting your skinny butt in jail!" He held two fingers close together and glared at Hortense.

She held her ground. "On what charge, Chief? You can't lock a person up for being neighborly!"

Large Bear returned and nodded at Sowinski. The crowd was dispersed by the big deputy. It took a while for everyone to leave, but soon the place was empty and Hortense had disappeared inside the house.

Nathan found her at the sink, washing up the coffee pot and utensils.

"Now what are you doing?" he asked her.

"You can't expect poor Maybelle to go to her reward and leave a sink full of dirty dishes, now can you? I'll just be a minute."

"OUT!" he shouted at her. "OUT!"

"Well, since you put it that way!" She opened the refrigerator and began putting her eggs back in her apron. "Maybelle, God rest her soul, won't be needing these either. I'll just take them back."

"OUT!"

Large Bear and Nathan sat at the kitchen table waiting on the funeral home to come, Large Bear doing his best to stifle the giggles in his throat. Nathan held his head in his hands.

Chapter 16

Skank Peterson sat in the chief's reception area with a stringer of fish dripping slimy water all over the floor.

Nathan's secretary, Genevieve was pitching a fit. "Skank, your fish smell bad, you smell bad and you're dripping water all over the floor," she said while she attempted to mop up, for the third time.

"Must you bring those fish in here?"

"I must," he said. "Steve and me were out fishing all morning and I thought Nathan could use these here fish. He done me a favor, and I'm grateful."

"I'm sure Marilyn will be thrilled," she muttered under her breath, recalling that the chief's wife was not fond of cooking. "He's had a busy morning and has not gotten back from lunch yet. if you want to leave, I'll tell him to call you."

"I heard about his busy morning. Rainey couldn't wait to tell me. And, no, I don't want to leave".

At that moment, Chief Sowinski walked into the office. Not seeing his visitor immediately, he addressed Genevieve. "Genevieve, what is that horrible smell, did you spill something?" He looked up and saw Skank and the fish, "Oh. . ."

Skank moved forward and held up the fish. "Me n' Steve caught a mess of drums. And I appreciate you helping to find them. So, I'm thanking you with these.'' He held the stringer out to the chief.

"Gee, thanks, Skank," he said while handing them to his secretary

She took them and left the room, hoping to find someplace to dump them and get them out of the office. When she got back Peterson was gone, and the chief was spraying Lysol around the office area.

"Where'd you put them?" he asked.

"I wrapped them in a plastic bag and put them in the dumpster out back. Was that okay?"

"Too bad we can't give them to somebody, because Marilyn hasn't a clue how to cook fish. And now we'll probably have every cat within twenty miles hanging around back there. But, yeah, I guess it was okay."

Sowinski's next visitor was Steve, who walked in and drew up a chair in front of the chief's desk. "Chief, something still bothers me about this New Orleans thing."

"Not surprising. By the way, how is Cassie doing?"

"She's still trying to shake off the effects of being sedated for three days running. But, she will be okay."

"So, what's on your mind?"

"The way this whole thing came down, I still get the feeling we have not caught the mastermind. This Andre person helped to procure the victims and no doubt this 'professor' person helped too. And there was a wealthy couple involved also, the Van Dams. Cassie was found in their home. I think for the most part, they provided a place to hide away the so called 'patients' until the time they were needed. And the household help was aware of it and kept watch. But I'm still having this nagging feeling that something was missing. I think everyone I mentioned was an accomplice, but some one individual put all this together, and they are still out there, claiming more victims. I'm sure of it."

Nathan sat back in his chair. "You're not thinking of going back, are you?"

"Are you serious? Suzanne would have my hide if I did! No, but I have some connections at the bureau in Washington and I think I'll give them a call. Maybe they can get to the bottom of it. What d'ya think?"

"Good idea. I'll make a few calls myself. Changing the subject, you goin' to Maybelle's funeral the day after tomorrow?"

"We are. I think everyone in town is, according to my wife. Maybelle baked sweets for every child in the cove. Has the coroner said what she died from?"

"Natural causes. She was diabetic, had a heart condition and was grossly overweight. It was inevitable."

Steve gave a low whistle, shaking his head. "Sooner or later, it would have all gotten her. What about Hortense and her neighbors? Any charges?"

Nathan took a bottle of water from his refrigerator, offered one to his visitor, and sat back down. "Not unless they've come up with a punishment for being a nuisance, and she's too old to send to her room without supper!"

Laughing, Steve got up to leave "Let's stay in touch, Chief.

***

Two afternoons later, Mariner's Chapel was full. Nearly the entire population of Beryl's Cove, turned out for Maybelle's funeral, with Hortense leading the mourners. Nathan and Marilyn, with their son Little Chief, slipped into the pew beside the entire Thomas clan. He leaned over towards Steve and began to whisper.

"The feds were already on the case. Said they'd been watching the activities for months and were getting nowhere. Until you came along, they had made no progress. By the way, John Hawthorne said to tell you 'hello.' He was lead investigator on this case ." He looked around, to make sure no one was being disturbed by their conversation. "You were right, Steve. The head man was missing. But they found out who it was and are in pursuit."

"Pursuit?" Steve raised his eyebrows at the news.

"Rochambeau. He was the head man. But he's on the lam, and may be headed here . . . to see you."

"Don't be silly, Nathan. Why would he come all this way for me?"

The chief nodded at Steve ,"Just be careful is all. I'll have your back.

***

As Pastor Kapas entered the sanctuary to begin the funeral, a certain police chief from New Orleans was

63

driving up the interstate, on his way to the North Carolina coast.

Chapter 17

The morning after Maybelle's funeral, Steve left early for the coffee shop with Dawg. The poor animal hadn't had a donut since he and Suzanne left for their trip. Suzanne went into the garden to work. The morning was pleasant, with just a hint of the springtime to come.

Dawg and his master were greeted with cheers and huzzahs, a high five from his brother Gene. Dawg jumped up into the booth, already salivating for the donut that was sure to come. When it appeared, he snatched it in midair and devoured it, licking his chops for more.

It was a stunned group of men who listened to Steve's version of their trip, with Gene adding in an update on Cassie's condition now. An hour later, another donut was tossed at Dawg and he and Steve left for home.

Cutting through the parking lot of the yacht club, the pair entered the Thomas' backyard. Suzanne's pruning shears lay on the ground and what looked like some kicked up turf was beside them. With no sign of his wife, Steve entered the house and looked in every room. Next he called Rainey and some of the neighbors, even dialing up Hortense, to ask if Suzanne was over there. She was not and Hortense fired off her shotgun for good measure.

Checking again for maybe a note from his wife, Steve went through virtually every drawer and nook looking for a clue as to where she might be. He went into the garage, both their car and motorcycle were there

Puzzled, he returned to the living room, and sat on the couch, petting the animals for comfort. It was then, he noticed Suzanne's purse on the floor next to the couch, one strap broken from it. He stared in disbelief for several seconds, then, dashed out the door, slamming it behind him, and ran toward the police station.

Genevieve looked up in surprise when she saw him headed into the chief's office. "He's in a meeting, Steve, you can't go in there." Too late. She was talking to his back.

***

Nathan made his excuses before hanging up on his conference call.

"I thought you were in a meeting", Steve said.

"I was, on a conference call. What in the world has gotten a hold of you anyway?"

"Suzanne's gone! Disappeared, Nathan. I can't find her anywhere. Nothing of hers is missing and I found her purse almost under the couch at home. One of the straps is broken." Steve was breathless, his face lined with worry. "This isn't like her at all."

Sowinski studied his friend, knowing full well that The Thomases were not prone to panic or snap

66

judgments. Steve never uttered a word unless he was sure of what he was saying. He was extremely levelheaded, until it came to his wife. He looked hard at Steve. "Tell me about it."

Meticulously, Steve told him about the mornings activities and finding the pruning shears and scuffed up grass in the backyard. He mentioned again the handbag he found and reiterated to the chief how he had called neighbors and friends. No-one had seen her.

"All vehicles accounted for?"

Steve nodded

Rubbing his chin, Nathan leaned forward in his chair. "Rochambeau ever show up?"

"You can't honestly think that man is behind this, can you?"

Nathan shrugged. "Stranger things have happened. Listen, Steve, if you want to kill a viper, how do you do it? You either take off the head or stab it in the heart, right?"

Steve twisted in his chair. "I'm not a viper!"

"Granted, but to him you are. She was with you throughout all of this, even helped to nail the guys, according to you. Anyone with half a brain can look at the two of you and see how much in love you are. So he stabbed you in the heart."

"I'll kill him!" Steve pounded one fist into another.

"Look," Nathan began, "it took him two days to get here, driving like fury. It will take him at least two days to get back, and he probably has Suzanne with him. Let me make some calls and see if we can track him. Go on home. I'll call you as soon as I know anything."

Steve was unmoved. "Not on your life, I'm staying right here in this chair until we know where he is. Then you and I are going after him." He crossed his arms and legs in a defiant gesture.

Nathan sighed, as he picked up the phone.

Chapter 18

Rochambeau drove his van like the devil himself was after him. His "cargo" in the back was heavily sedated and, as he approached Biloxi, Mississippi, he picked up speed. He had "customers" waiting for a new kidney and lung. He didn't want to disappoint them. And he marveled at how easy it had been to take the fetching Mrs. Thomas. Her organs would bring a pretty penny to the coffers.

He glanced back at her, smiled and picked up his speed to nearly 80 mph. Maybe, he thought, he'd have a little "recreation" with her before turning her over to the surgeon.

***

Officers Grady Gardner and Marshall Baumont were on patrol. They were driving along Highway 90 just outside of Biloxi when a speeding van literally whizzed by their unmarked vehicle. Grady turned on the bright lights and cranked up the siren. His partner called it in and simultaneously heard about the area wide APB put out for Rochambeau and the van he had stolen in Atlanta.

The chase went on for several minutes before the officers were able to pull up alongside and motion for the driver to pull over. Both officers approached the van, one on either side of it. Rochambeau rolled his window down and chuckled as they approached.

"Sorry, officers, I know I was speeding, but my wife's very ill and I'm rushing her to the hospital."

"That her in the back? What's her name?" Grady shone his flashlight into the van, illuminating Suzanne. "She always sleep that soundly, Mr. . . .?"

"Gibson, Frank Gibson. Her name's Kathy, Kathy Gibson. He pulled out his driver's license, a well-done fake with his picture on it and the name Frank Gibson.

"Well Mr. Gibson, you won't find the hospital you're looking for on this stretch of road. You need to follow the signs out on the interstate."

As Grady stalled the man, Marshall walked up to him and spoke in low tones. "Not sleeping. Drugged."

Grady stepped away from the van and drew his gun, "Step out of the vehicle please, sir."

Rochambeau glared at the policemen and very quickly stepped on the gas, driving as fast as he could to get away.

Returning to their car, the two officers scrambled to give chase. They pulled away, Grady driving, and Marshall calling in for backup.

Racing up Highway 90, the cops looked in horror as Rochambeau seemed to lose control, overturned, and careened into the Gulf, where the tide was swiftly pulling his van out to sea.

Both officers ran after the van, swimming as hard as they could with heavy equipment on, trying desperately to reach the bouncing vehicle that was now being tossed about on the waves and in danger of sinking.

As they fought the current, Rochambeau's dead body bobbed on the waves

Chapter 19

Nathan Sowinski hung up the phone and rubbed his unshaven chin.

True to his word, Steve had stayed in the chief's office overnight, waiting to hear from anyone about his wife. Nathan worried that sitting all night in that chair would make Steve unable to move this morning. He himself stayed too in sympathy, sleeping in a recliner last night, making him now stiff as a board. Now, hearing this tragic phone call, he didn't know how to approach Steve. The man adored his wife. This news would certainly unhinge him . . . maybe.

He walked over to his friend, woke him gently and handed him a cup of coffee. "Just heard from the police in Biloxi, Mississippi. During a police chase, Rochambeau crashed the van and careened into the Gulf with Suzanne in the back of a stolen van, drugged. Rochambeau is dead."

The color drained from Steve's face. "Suzanne?"

"A little banged up, but alive and in the hospital recovering. She was nearly drowned and suffering from shock, when the two officers found her and pulled her from the sinking van. She will be all right. With Rochambeau dead, and Suzanne drugged, tragically, we'll never know the full story. I'll get Genevieve to make some travel arrangements. I'd like to go with you, Steve, and thank the officers who saved her life—one cop to another, you know."

Steve stood up, stretched, and grabbed Nathan by the shoulder. "Sure. Let's go."

"Now? Without a shower or change of clothes?"

"This is my wife we're talking about, Chief. Get the lead out and let's go!"

As Steve marched them both from the office the chief was able to shout for Genevieve to call his wife and tell her where they were going and that he'd be back as soon as he could.

Once out the back door by the dumpster as they tried to tuck in their shirts and make themselves as presentable as possible, Steve sniffed the air and saw all the cats circling the dumpster meowing loudly. "What in God's name is that horrible odor and where did all these cats come from?"

"Get in the car. It's a long story. I'll tell you while we head for the airport."

Chapter 20

Suzanne had been taken to Keesler Air Force Base Hospital because it was close, their trauma unit was unbeatable, and Steve's FBI friend knew that—with Steve's military credentials—she would have no trouble getting admitted.

Genevieve had made travel arrangements for them and, after landing on a private airstrip, a rental car was waiting for them. They raced to Keesler.

Finding a parking place rather easily, the two men hurried inside, found the trauma unit and inquired about Suzanne.

"You mean the Jane Doe who was brought in by the Biloxi PD?"

Exasperated, Steve gave her a hard look. "Yeah, but she's not a 'Jane Doe.' Her name is Suzanne Thomas and she's my wife. Where is she?"

He started off down the hall before the nurse could announce anything more than her room number and, finding her room, burst in and embraced her.

She smiled at him and looked askance at his appearance. "I thought the grunge look was passe, Mr. Thomas, but you obviously have brought it back. And with flair, I must say. I'm fine. Now get me out of here and take me home."

"With pleasure, ma'am," he said, while grabbing her clothes and disconnecting all her IVs.

Nathan entered the room just then, and asked what they thought they were doing.

"What's it look like, Chief? We're going home."

"Doesn't she have to be discharged by a doctor or something first?"

"We are discharging her." Seeing his wife standing by the bed, he said, "Let's go!"

Nathan shook his head in amusement at the pair. "I'm ready, but I would like to go and thank the police officers who got her here. Wanna come along?"

"I'm not leaving Suzanne, but wait—" He took out his checkbook, wrote out a check and gave it to Sowinski. "Here, give this to the fellas at the station, and tell them to buy themselves a celebration with it. From me, with my thanks."

Nathan whistled at the amount, gave a tip-of-the-hat gesture, and spoke once again. "Meet you in the car." Then he left, just as the head nurse was entering the room.

"What's going on here, sir?"

"We're leaving. I'm taking my wife home, if you'll step aside and let us pass."

He tried guiding Suzanne around the woman but she held her ground.

"I'm afraid that's not possible, Mr. Thomas. She has not seen the doctor today or been properly discharged. Now, I'll thank you both to turn around and get her back in bed." She stood still with her hands on her hips, glaring at Steve.

"Not on your life, lady! Here." He picked up Suzanne, dropped a business card into the nurse's hand and almost ran down the hall to the elevator. He shouted out to her, as the doors closed around them, "Send me a bill!"

Still carrying his wife, they made it to the rental as Nathan pulled away. Two security guards ran after them but were unable to catch up. In twenty minutes they were back at the airstrip, lifting off for home. The three of them waved to the folks on the ground, just as they climbed higher, Suzanne laughing at the image of them being chased.

"Your he-man antics made it impossible for me to go to the station to thank the men, but I'll send a note with your check to everyone for you."

The Thomases, sitting entwined on a settee in their private chartered jet, only nodded.

Chapter 21

Nothing beats sleeping in your own bed and Suzanne fell into it with glee once they were home.

While deplaning in Wilmington, Steve had thanked Nathan for his help. He followed Suzanne's lead by getting into bed for a good night's sleep.

Rainey was at the door the next morning before they could finish breakfast. She burst into the kitchen like the fireball she was, hugged Steve and went directly to Suzanne.

"Girlfriend, I've been so worried about you. Skank's been thumping his chest every minute you've been away." She pulled up a chair, poured herself a cup of coffee and sat down. "Now, tell me all the good stuff."

Steve chuckled at their friend and stood up. "You beauties have at it. I think I'll take Dawg and go on to the coffee shop. Good seeing you again, Rainey."

As usual the coffee shop was full, the chatter going strong. Dawg and Steve slid easily into their favorite booth across from Nathan and Gene. Moments later, here came Bullet Head, who forced himself into the booth with Dawg nearly in his lap.

"Wassup, Swabbi? Have fun in the crescent city or what?" His loud guffaw could be heard all over the shop. "Seriously," he slapped Steve on the back, "Happy it all worked out well." Looking at Gene he asked, "Girls okay?"

Taking a sip of coffee, Gene nodded, put his cup down and replied, "Yeah, I grounded them for life though." He smiled at his brother, "I know, but it sounds good, right?"

As the town woke up and began to stir around, the tourists woke up as well and drifted into the cove, going in one shop after another,+

***

Easter was fast approaching and, much to Pastor Kappas' chagrin, the yacht club scheduled a dance for the Saturday before. Nathan's brother Paul and his band were booked to play for it.

Four days later at the dance, the Thomases were approached by Chief Sowinski. As he sat down he nodded to the women. Bending near Steve, he barely spoke: "I heard from your FBI buddy, this Hawthorne guy. They have closed the book on this case after finally arresting all the principals. You and the misses want to finally put it to rest, come by my office Monday morning and I'll fill you in." Nodding to Gene and Cassie, he added, "Them too."

Nathan stood up, made a half bow to Suzanne, Cassie and Rainey, turned and escorted his wife to a table.

At the next slow number, the whole group stood up to dance. Staying until the last moment, and beyond, the Thomas table hung around to catch Paul and Ginny and have a word with them.

Traditionally, the yacht club served a huge Easter morning breakfast buffet beginning at 7 am. And, since Pastor Kappas approved of the early rising church crowd, they often attended too.

All of the group, including Paul and his band members, decided that they would partake of the buffet at 8:30 the next morning. Bidding one another good night, the party broke up and everyone departing to their home, Paul and Ginny staying with his brother and wife.

Chapter 22

The Monday after Eater is a holiday in North Carolina, but not for the police. Police Chief Nathan Sowinski sat in his office that morning, waiting on the two Thomas couples. He gave Genevieve the day off. Sipping his coffee from a thermos, he shuffled papers around on his desk. He had two deputies on duty patrolling the town. They had reported that all was well. It usually was in Beryl's Cove.

As his guests arrived, he stood up and offered them chairs. "Glad everyone could come in this morning. Here. I've made copies of this report for each of you." After handing out the reports, he sat down again. "As you can see, there was a rather extensive chain of command in the 'harvesting' operations. Jacque Rochambeau was not the head. Dr. Joel Ashlen is—or was—a research doctor at the University there. He recruited all the others.

"This doctor thought it would be a kick to recruit all his so called 'patients' for organ donors and bring lots of money into his project at the same time. He's been picked up, by the way. Now, we come to the 'professor,' who was in the position to scout out healthy, young 'donors.' He'd pass their name along to Andre at his restaurant and then invite the kids to the restaurant for dinner as a treat. Being college kids, they were always looking for a freebie anywhere. Once there, Andre would drug them, and

Rochambeau would have them picked up on some trumped up charge and turn them over to the albino. Once they were blind drunk on whatever substance they were given, they'd carry the victim to the cabin in the bayou and wait for the call to bring them to Dr. Ashlen's clinic, where he would perform rudimentary surgery. Then they'd end up at the Van Dams' for 'recovery.'"

Steve and Gene listened and, shaking their heads, seemed to be stunned beyond words.

Nathan gave Cassie a tissue to wipe tears away. He continued: "In the case of your nieces, they were simply in the wrong place at the wrong time. Andre saw them as perfect specimens, and identical yet. So they took Cassie. The plan was to go back after Susie once her sister had been moved out of the Van Dams' place. Because they were backed up, so to speak, with 'patients,' they took Cassie there first to wait. She was, as you know, heavily sedated. So she couldn't or wouldn't go for help .Thank goodness her sister did. Something went wrong though and two people were overdosed and died."

Cassie was crying blowing her nose. She looked at the chief and asked, "Why didn't some of those other kids, the lucky ones who lived, why didn't they go to the police?"

"Because," the chief handed her another tissue, "Rochambeau *was* the police, and he was in on it. No, probably out of embarrassment, they simply sucked it up and went on as best they could. The ones who had

had a lung removed, more than likely, went home. That is a serious thing to undergo. Anything else?"

Suzanne had buried her head in her hands, but now she questioned why this so called scheme was hatched in the first place. "It's beyond the pale," she added.

"Money. If you were incapacitated with kidney disease or dying from COPD, as the waiting patients were, wouldn't you go anywhere and pay anything to get well again? They never had a clue. The FBI is currently talking to the folks on the waiting list. Believe me, if you were that sick, you wouldn't care if it was a legal or ethical procedure or not. Trust me."

Nathan seemed undone by it all. He looked at his folded hands in his lap.

Steve could hardly speak. "So much for the Hippocratic oath: 'First, do no harm.' Suzanne?"

"You all were getting too close. Rochambeau had to act. His part in the scheme was close to being divulged by Officer Delaney and Mother Rosalie and he knew they had been talking to you. He had to act. Both of them are in protective custody now, too. Thought you'd like to know. Your buddy, Hawthorne, finished the investigation and thanks to the information you and I gave him, the FBI was able to run it all down. You might want to give him a call."

Nodding at Nathan, the two couples left the office in silence and, embracing, left the station to go to their individual homes. Steve and Suzanne had walked the two blocks to the station. So hand-in-hand, they began to walk back.

"What now?" she asked.

"I'm going to buy a dump truck, the biggest one I can find."

They stopped in the middle of the road and Suzanne gave a raised eyebrow look to her husband. "A dump truck? Why did you decide to buy a dump truck?"

"It seemed like a good idea at the time." He smiled at her, took her hand and they began to walk again.

"What do you plan to put in it, Steve?"

"All my love for you. And I'll drive it everywhere with me,"

She stared at him for the longest time, then—right in the in the middle of the road—they embraced.

Epilogue—How the Pets See It

Dawg lay in his usual spot, right in the middle of the sunbeam coming in through the patio door. His soft dog wheezing was really annoying Elvis. So the feline decided to wake him up. The cat jumped on Dawg and began to softly chew on the bulldog's ear. Dawg rolled over onto his side, throwing Elvis to the floor.

"Hey," the cat protested, "you dumb dog, you need to wake up so we can have meeting."

"What kind of a meeting and who put you in charge?" Dawg began to lick himself.

"Cut that out. It's disgusting! I'm in charge because I'm a cat, and all cats are in charge. Haven't you learned anything living with me?" He glared at Dawg through slitted, half-closed eyes.

"Now, to begin with, we need to prevent Dad from getting involved in these messes he is so prone to get involved in. And Mom is no slouch either. So I have a plan. I want you to run outside and get yourself run over by a car. Doesn't need to be a big one. Even just a slight bump will do. And they will feel so guilty they'll never leave us again,! Go on, go, I'll hold your spot in the sunbeam for you," said the cat as he stretched out in the sun, purring.

Dawg flattened his already flat ears and nudged the cat. He was angry and added a deep bulldog growl as he did so.

"Hey, cut it out. Okay, okay, don't get hit by a car. It was just a suggestion, you dumb dog."

The bulldog charged, ramming into Elvis and pushing him up against the patio door. "And, another thing, I am not dumb. At least I'm house broken. You still have to use a litter box because you're too stupid to whine and scratch when you want to go out. Now, who's the dummy?"

"Let go of me fat boy. I have another plan."

Dawg rolled off of Elvis, letting him up from where he had pushed him. He sat staring at the cat. Finally he slid down on his belly and cocked his head. "Oh all right. Tell me your plan—and it had better be better than your first suggestion. If it isn't, you best be the one who gets hit by a car. I'll even help!"

Shaking himself off, Elvis began to clean himself, all the while, keeping an eye on the Bulldog.

"Well?"

"I'm thinking!" He continued with his grooming. Hearing his parental humans upstairs, he quickly got up and sat down next to Dawg, hissing into his ear. "Here's what we do, see. We begin to show we are suffering from separation anxiety. So bad, in fact, that Mom and Dad can't leave us or pawn us off on Rainey and Skank and that infernally obnoxious setter they have. Boy, what a pris pot she is."

"I know," Dawg added. "I myself prefer the company of their goat, Dolly. Now *there's* what I call a real pet. And she stays outside most of the time." He cast a glaring, mean look at Elvis. "I'm only going along with this because I want to keep Mom and Dad safe and out of danger."

Hearing their parent humans coming downstairs, the animals went into pitiful mode, whining, and circling on their feet, earning themselves each a scratch behind the ears. This caused Elvis to begin purring exceptionally loudly, a smirk on his face.

Dawg went and laid down on the small mat in front of the stove, effectively blocking it. He smirked back at Elvis and hissed, "Show off."

Last word from the Thomas pets? Not on your life!

www.ingramcontent.com/pod-product-compliance
Lightning Source LLC
Chambersburg PA
CBHW070942250626

47159CB00009B/3355